Mikado Enterprises, L.L.C.

(an adaptation for the modern stage)

by Don Bliss

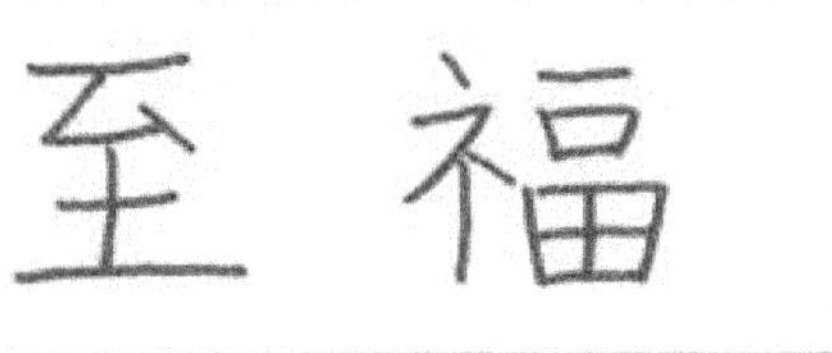

Original version of "The Mikado"
by William S. Gilbert
Music by Sir Arthur Sullivan

Legal Stuff

Important Note

All producers of "Mikado Enterprises, L.L.C." shall announce the names of Arthur S. Sullivan and W.S. Gilbert as the original author and composer of this work, and shall credit Don Bliss with the adaptation of the work on all programs, posters, webpages and other printed matter such as paid advertising under the producer's control. The credit to the authors/adaptor shall be not less than fifty percent (50%) of the size of type used for the title of the play. Said billing shall appear on seperate lines following the title of the play and shall appear in the following form:

(Name of Producer)
presents

Mikado Enterprises, L.L.C.

A modern adaptation of
"The Mikado"
by W.S. Gilbert and Sir Arthur Sullivan
Adaptation by Don Bliss

original stage production by the Viking Theater Company

Printed in U.S.A.
ISBN 978-0-557-23254-3

Musical Numbers
Act I

1. "If you want to know who we are" (Nanki-Poo, Men)
2. "A Wand'ring Driver I" (Nanki-Poo and Men)
3. "Our Great CEO, virtuous man" (Pish-Tush and Men)
4. "Young man, despair" (Pooh-Bah, Nanki-Poo and Pish-Tush)
5. "Behold the VP Human Resources" (Ko-Ko and Men)

5a. "As some day it may happen" (Ko-Ko and Men)

6. "Comes a train of little ladies" (Girls)
7. "Three little maids from the Pool are we" (Yum-Yum, Peep-Bo, Pitti-Sing, and Girls)
8. "So please you, Sir, we much regret" (Yum-Yum, Peep-Bo, Pitti-Sing, Pooh-Bah, and Girls)
9. "Were you not to Ko-Ko plighted" (Yum-Yum and Nanki-Poo)
10. "I am so proud" (Pooh-Bah, Ko-Ko and Pish-Tush)
11. Finale Act I (Ensemble)

    "With aspect stern and gloomy stride"
    "The threatened cloud has passed away"
    "Your revels cease!"
    "Oh fool, that fleest my hallowed joys!"
    "For he's going to marry Yum-Yum"
    "The hour of gladness"
    "O ni! bikkuri shakkuri to!"
    "Ye torrents roar!"

Musical Numbers

Act II

12. "Braid the maiden hair" (Pitti-Sing and Girls)
13. "The sun whose rays are all ablaze" (Yum-Yum)
14. "Brightly dawns our wedding day" (Yum-Yum, Pitti-Sing, Nanki-Poo and Pish-Tush)
15. "Here's a how-de-do" (Yum-Yum, Nanki-Poo and Ko-Ko)
16. "Mi-ya Sa-ma...."(CEO, Katisha, Chorus)
17. "See how the Fates their gifts allot" (CEO, Pitti-Sing, Pooh-Bah, Ko-Ko and Katisha)
18. "The flowers that bloom in the spring" (Nanki-Poo, Ko-Ko, Yum-Yum, Pitti-Sing, and Pooh-Bah)
19. "Alone, and yet alive" (Katisha)
20. "Willow, tit-willow" (Ko-Ko)
21. "There is beauty in the bellow of the blast" (Katisha and Ko-Ko)
22. "For he's gone and married Yum-Yum"
    "The threatened cloud has passed away" (Ensemble)

Setting

ACT I.—The Boardroom of Mikado Enterprises, LLC

ACT II.—The Women's Washroom, The Boardroom

The original version of "The Mikado" was first produced at the Savoy Theatre on March 14, 1885.

The adaptation published here was performed at Wareham High School, Wareham, Massachusetts on May 6, 2009. The following actors played the adapted roles:

THE CEO – Andrea Couto
NANKI-POO – Eric Balboni
KO-KO – Alex Couto
POOH-BAH – Chris Silva
PISH-TUSH – Kayla Rounds / Maroby Walls
YUM-YUM – Bunny Bassett
PITTI-SING – Brittany Nyman
PEEP-BO – Eleasha Schmidt
KATISHA – Kassandra Peterson

Dramatis Personae

THE CEO	*(of Mikado Enterprises, LLC)*
NANKI-POO	*(his Son, disguised as the IPS delivery man and in love with Yum-Yum).*
KO-KO	*(Vice President in charge of Human Resources (hiring and firing - mostly firing))*
POOH-BAH	*(Vice President in charge of Everything Else).*
PISH-TUSH	*(a security guard).*
YUM-YUM	*(a secretary, beloved of Koko)*
PITTI-SING	*(a secretary and friend of Yum Yum)*
PEEP-BO	*(a secretary)*
KATISHA	*(the elderly cleaning lady, in love with Nanki-Poo).*
CHORUS	*(Board members, computer professionals, secretaries, security guards, etc.)*

ACT 1

SCENE.—The Boardroom of Mikado Enterprises, LLC.. Board members are filing in for a meeting.

CHORUS OF BUSINESSMEN.

IF YOU WANT TO KNOW WHO ARE WE,
WE ARE BUSINESSMEN OF JAPAN:
EACH WITH HIS OWN BLACKBERRY--
AND EACH WITH RETIREMENT PLAN,
WE KEEP UP WITH MARKET NEWS:
IN PRADA AND GUCCI SHOES--
OUR STOCK OPTIONS NEVER LOSE, OH!

IF YOU THINK WE ARE WORKED BY STRINGS,
LIKE A JAPANESE MARIONETTE,
YOU DON'T UNDERSTAND THESE THINGS:
IT IS SIMPLY OUR ETIQUETTE.
PERHAPS YOU SUPPOSE THIS THRONG
CAN'T KEEP IT UP ALL DAY LONG?
IF THAT'S YOUR IDEA, YOU'RE WRONG, OH!

[*Enter Nanki-Poo in great excitement. He carries a stack of parcels in his arms.*]

RECIT.--NANKI-POO.

GENTLEMEN, I PRAY YOU TELL ME
WHERE A SECRETARY WORKETH,
NAMED YUM-YUM, THE AIDE OF KO-KO?
IN PITY SPEAK, OH SPEAK I PRAY YOU!

SECURITY GUARD. Why, who are you who ask this question?
NANKI-POO. Come gather round me, and I'll tell you.

SONG and CHORUS--NANKI-POO.

A WANDERING DRIVER I--
A THING OF SHREDS AND PATCHES,
OF BALLADS, SONGS AND SNATCHES,
AND DREAMY LULLABY!

MY CATALOGUE IS LONG,
THROUGH EVERY PASSION RANGING,
AND TO YOUR HUMOURS CHANGING
I TUNE MY SUPPLE SONG!
ARE YOU IN SENTIMENTAL MOOD?
I'LL SIGH WITH YOU,
OH, SORROW, SORROW!
ON MAIDEN'S COLDNESS DO YOU BROOD?
I'LL DO SO, TOO--
OH, SORROW, SORROW!
I'LL CHARM YOUR WILLING EARS
WITH SONGS OF LOVERS' FEARS,
WHILE SYMPATHETIC TEARS
MY CHEEKS BEDEW--
OH, SORROW, SORROW!

BUT IF EXPEDITED SENTIMENT IS WANTED,
I'VE EXPEDITED BALLADS CUT AND DRIED;
FOR WHERE'ER THE COMP'NY BANNER MAY BE PLANTED,
ALL OF THOSE FEDEX BANNERS ARE DEFIED!
OUR WARRIORS, IN BROWN-CLAD RANKS ASSEMBLED,
NEVER QUAIL—THEY'RE ALWAYS FIRST AT EACH ADDRESS--
AND I SHOULDN'T BE SURPRISED IF OTHERS TREMBLED
BEFORE THE MIGHTY TRUCKS OF IPS!

CHORUS. WE SHOULDN'T BE SURPRISED, ETC.

NANKI-POO. AND IF YOU SHIP TO A PLACE OVERSEAS,
WE'LL HEAVE THE PACKAGE ROUND,
WITH A YO HEAVE HO, FOR FRA-GI-LI-TIES,
WE TOSS 'EM A-ROUND AS ROUGH AS WE PLEASE,
HURRAH FOR THE OUTWARD BOUND!

CHORUS. YO-HO--HEAVE HO--
HURRAH FOR THE OUTWARD BOUND!
TO LAY AROUND IN AN AIRPORT LOUNGE
MAY TICKLE SOME MAILMAN'S TASTE,
BUT THE HAPPIEST HOUR A DRIVER SEES
IS WHEN HE'S DOWN
AT A SEAPORT TOWN,
WITH A BARMAID ON HIS KNEES, YO HO!
AND HIS ARM AROUND HER WAIST!
CHORUS. THEN MAN THE BROWN TRUCKS--OFF WE GO,
AS THE DISPATCH SENDS US ROUND,
WITH A YO HEAVE HO,
AND A RUM BELOW,
HURRAH FOR THE OUTWARD BOUND!

A WANDERING DRIVER I, ETC.

[*Enter Pish-Tush.*]

PISH-TUSH. And what may be your business with Yum-Yum?

NANKI-POO. I'll tell you. A year ago I toiled in the mail room. It was my duty to take the cart round with deliveries. While discharging this delicate office, I saw Yum-Yum. We loved each other at once, but she was betrothed to her boss Ko-Ko, a programmer, and I saw that my cause was hopeless. Overwhelmed with despair, I quit the company. Imagine my delight when I heard, a month ago, that Ko-Ko was about to be terminated for having an office romance! I hurried back at once, in the hope of finding Yum-Yum at liberty to listen to my protestations.

PISH-TUSH. It is true that Ko-Ko was terminated for having an office romance, but he was promoted to the exalted position of Vice President of Human Resources, under the following remarkable circumstances:

SONG--PISH-TUSH and CHORUS.

OUR GREAT CEO, VIRTUOUS ONE,
WHEN HE BEGAN OUR FIRM TO RUN,
RESOLVED TO TRY
A PLAN WHEREBY
YOUNG MEN MIGHT BEST BE HIRED.
SO HE DECREED, IN WORDS SUCCINCT,
THAT ALL WHO FLIRTED, LEERED OR WINKED
(UNLESS CONNUBIALLY LINKED),
SHOULD RIGHT AWAY BE FIRED.
AND I EXPECT YOU'LL ALL AGREE
THAT HE WAS RIGHT TO SO DECREE.
AND I AM RIGHT,
AND YOU ARE RIGHT,
AND ALL IS RIGHT AS RIGHT CAN BE!

CHORUS. AND YOU ARE RIGHT. AND WE ARE RIGHT, ETC

THIS STEM DECREE, YOU'RE SMART TO LEARN,
CAUSED GREAT DISMAY THROUGHOUT THE FIRM!
FOR YOUNG AND OLD
AND SHY AND BOLD
WERE EQUALLY AFFECTED.
THE YOUTH WHO WINKED A ROVING EYE,
OR BREATHED A NON-CONNUBIAL SIGH,
WAS THEREUPON CONDEMNED TO CRY--
HE USUALLY OBJECTED.
AND YOU'LL ALLOW, AS I EXPECT,
THAT HE WAS RIGHT TO SO OBJECT.
AND I AM RIGHT,
AND YOU ARE RIGHT,
AND EVERYTHING IS QUITE CORRECT!

CHORUS. AND YOU ARE RIGHT, AND WE ARE RIGHT, ETC.

AND SO WE STRAIGHT AWAY DID SPY
THIS PROGRAMMER WITH ROVING EYE
WHOSE JOB WAS NEXT
ON SOME PRETEXT
CONDEMNED TO BE THROWN OFF,
AND MADE HIM 'H.R.', FOR WE SAID,
"WHO'S NEXT TO BE TERMINATED
CANNOT HIMSELF ANOTHER SHED
UNTIL HE'S LAID HIMSELF OFF."
AND WE ARE RIGHT, I THINK YOU'LL SAY,
TO ARGUE IN THIS KIND OF WAY;
AND I AM RIGHT,
AND YOU ARE RIGHT,
AND ALL IS RIGHT--TOO-LOORAL-LAY!

CHORUS. AND YOU ARE RIGHT, AND WE ARE RIGHT, ETC.
[*Exit Chorus. Enter Pooh-Bah.*]

NANKI-POO. Ko-Ko, the Programmer, Vice President of Human Resources! Why, that's the highest job one could attain!

POOH-BAH. It is. Our logical CEO, seeing no moral difference between the thoughtful man who does the employee evaluations and the cruel one who fires the poor performers has rolled the two jobs into one, and every boss is now his own Turk.

NANKI-POO. But how good of you (for I see that you are a manager of the highest rank) to condescend to tell all this to me, a mere delivery man!

POOH-BAH. Don't mention it. I am, in point of fact, a particularly haughty and exclusive person, with an MBA from Bristol Community College. Consequently, my family pride is something inconceivable. I can't help it. I was born sneering. But I struggle hard to overcome this defect. I mortify my pride continually. When all the great officers of the Board of Directors resigned in a body because they were too proud to serve under an ex-Programmer, did I not unhesitatingly accept all their posts at once?

PISH-TUSH. And the salaries attached to them? You did.

POOH-BAH. It is consequently my degrading duty to serve this upstart as Chief Financial Officer, Head Legal Counsel, Head of Security, Keeper of the Key to the Executive Washroom, Refiller of the Lobby Candy Machine, OSHA Compliance Officer, Chaplain to the Board, and Principal of Wareham High School, both acting and elect, all rolled into one. And at a salary! A Pooh-Bah paid for his services! I a salaried minion! But I do it! It revolts me, but I do it!

NANKI-POO. And it does you credit.

POOH-BAH. But I don't stop at that. I go and dine with middle-class people on reasonable terms. I dance at cheap suburban parties for a moderate fee. I accept refreshment at any hands, however lowly. I also retail corporate secrets at a very low figure. For instance, any further information about Yum-Yum would come under the head of a corporate secret. (*Nanki-Poo takes his hint, and gives him money.*) (*Aside.*) Another insult and, I think, a light one!

SONG--POOH-BAH with NANKI-POO and PISH-TUSH.

YOUNG MAN, DESPAIR,
LIKEWISE GO TO,
YUM-YUM THE FAIR
YOU MUST NOT WOO.
IT WILL NOT DO:
I'M SORRY FOR YOU,
SO VERY FRUSTRATED BY THESE COURSES!
THIS VERY DAY
FROM WORK YUM-YUM
WILL WEND HER WAY,
AND HOMEWARD COME,
WITH BEAT OF DRUM
AND A RUM-TUM-TUM,
TO WED THE VP –HUMAN RESOURCES!
AND THE BRASS WILL CRASH,
AND THE TRUMPETS BRAY,
AND THEY'LL CUT A DASH
ON THEIR WEDDING DAY.
THEY'LL GALLOP AWAY, ON WHITE HORSES,
MRS. YUM YUM HUMAN RESOURCES!

NANKI-POO. AND POOH-BAH. AND THE BRASS WILL CRASH, ETC.

IT'S A HOPELESS CASE,
AS YOU MAY SEE,
AND IN YOUR PLACE
AWAY I'D FLEE;
BUT DON'T BLAME ME--
I'M SORRY TO BE
OF YOUR PLEASURE A DIMINUTIONER.
THEY'LL VOW THEIR PACT
EXTREMELY SOON,
IN POINT OF FACT
THIS AFTERNOON.
HER HONEYMOON

WITH THAT BUFFOON
AT SEVEN COMMENCES, SO YOU SHUN HER!

ALL. AND THE BRASS WILL CRASH, ETC.
[*Exit Pish-Tush.*]

RECITATIVE. NANKI-POO and POOH-BAH.

NANKI-POO. AND I HAVE JOURNEYED FOR A MONTH, OR NEARLY,
TO LEARN THAT YUM-YUM, WHOM I LOVE SO DEARLY,
THIS DAY TO KO-KO IS TO BE UNITED!
POOH-BAH. THE FACT APPEARS TO BE AS YOU'VE RECITED:
BUT HERE HE COMES, EQUIPPED AS SUITS HIS STATION;
HE'LL GIVE YOU ANY FURTHER INFORMATION.
[*Exit Pooh-Bah and Nanki-Poo. Enter Chorus of men, carrying Ko-Ko on their shoulders.*]

SONG--KO-KO AND MEN

CHORUS. BEHOLD THE VP –HUMAN RESOURCES!
A PERSONAGE OF NOBLE RANK AND TITLE--
A DIGNIFIED AND POTENT OFFICER,
WHOSE FUNCTIONS ARE PARTICULARLY VITAL!
OF COURSE, OF COURSE,
IT'S THE VP –HUMAN RESOURCES!!

SOLO--KO-KO.

TAKEN FROM THE SURE PINK SLIP
BY A SET OF CURIOUS CHANCES;
OVER MANY I DID SKIP,
ON MY OWN RECOGNIZANCES;
WAFTED BY A FAVOURING GALE
AS ONE SOMETIMES IS IN TRANCES,
TO A HEIGHT THAT FEW CAN SCALE,
SAVE BY LONG AND WEARY DANCES;
SURELY, NEVER HAD A MALE

UNDER SUCH LIKE CIRCUMSTANCES
SO ADVENTUROUS A TALE,
WHICH MAY RANK WITH MOST ROMANCES.

CHORUS. OF COURSE, OF COURSE,
IT'S THE VP –HUMAN RESOURCES!!

KO-KO. Gentlemen, I'm much touched by this reception. I can only trust that by strict attention to duty I shall ensure a continuance of those favors which it will ever be my study to deserve. If I should ever be called upon to act professionally, I am happy to think that there will be no difficulty in finding plenty of people whose loss will be a distinct gain to the company at large.

SONG--KO-KO with CHORUS OF MEN.

AS SOME DAY IT MAY HAPPEN
THAT A VICTIM MUST BE FOUND,
I'VE GOT A LITTLE LIST--I'VE GOT A LITTLE LIST
OF SOCIETY OFFENDERS
WHO MIGHT WELL BE UNDERGROUND,
AND WHO NEVER WOULD BE MISSED—
WHO NEVER WOULD BE MISSED!
THERE'S THE PESTILENTIAL NUISANCES
WHO WRITE FOR AUTOGRAPHS--
ALL PEOPLE WHO HAVE FLABBY HANDS
AND IRRITATING LAUGHS--
ALL TEACHERS WHO ARE UP IN AGE,
AND QUIZ YOU JUST LIKE THAT!--
ALL PERSONS WHO IN SHAKING HANDS,
SHAKE HANDS WITH YOU LIKE THAT--
AND ALL THIRD PERSONS WHO ON SPOILING
TÊTE-Á-TÊTES INSIST
THEY'D NONE OF 'EM BE MISSED —
THEY'D NONE OF 'EM BE MISSED

CHORUS. HE'S GOT 'EM ON THE LIST--HE'S GOT 'EM ON THE LIST;

AND THEY'LL NONE OF 'EM BE MISSED—
THEY'LL NONE OF 'EM BE MISSED.

KO_KO.
THERE'S THE FOX NEWS COMMENTATOR,
AND THE OTHERS OF HIS RACE,
AND AROMA-THERAPISTS--I'VE GOT THEM ON THE LIST!
AND THE PEOPLE WHO SMOKE CIGARETTES
AND PUFF THEM IN YOUR FACE,
THEY NEVER WOULD BE MISSED—
THEY NEVER WOULD BE MISSED!
THEN THE IDIOT WHO PRAISES,
WITH ENTHUSIASTIC TONE,
ALL CENTURIES BUT THIS,
AND EVERY COUNTRY BUT HIS OWN;
AND THE LADY FROM THE PROVINCES,
WHO DRESSES LIKE A GUY,
AND WHO "DOESN'T THINK SHE TWITTERS,
BUT WOULD RATHER LIKE TO TRY";
AND THAT SINGULAR ANOMALY,
THE LADY NOVELIST--
I DON'T THINK SHE'D BE MISSED—
I'M SURE SHE'D NOT HE MISSED!

CHORUS. HE'S GOT HER ON THE LIST—
HE'S GOT HER ON THE LIST;
AND I DON'T THINK SHE'LL BE MISSED—
I'M SURE SHE'LL NOT BE MISSED!
KO-KO.
AND THAT NOT SO CLEVER NUISANCE,
WHO JUST NOW IS RATHER RIFE,
THE LATE-NIGHT HUMORIST--I'VE GOT HIM ON THE LIST!
ALL FUNNY FELLOWS, COMIC MEN,
AND CLOWNS OF PRIVATE LIFE--

THEY'D NONE OF 'EM BE MISSED—
THEY'D NONE OF 'EM BE MISSED.
AND CHEATING POLITICIANS
OF A COMPROMISING KIND,
SUCH AS--WHAT D'YE CALL HIM--THING'EM-BOB,
AND LIKEWISE-- NEVER-MIND,
AND 'ST--'ST--'ST--AND WHAT'S-HIS-NAME,
AND ALSO YOU-KNOW- WHO--
THE TASK OF FILLING UP THE BLANKS
I'D RATHER LEAVE TO YOU.
BUT IT REALLY DOESN'T MATTER
WHOM YOU PUT UPON THE LIST,
FOR THEY'D NONE OF 'EM BE MISSED—
THEY'D NONE OF 'EM BE MISSED!

CHORUS. YOU MAY PUT 'EM ON THE LIST—
YOU MAY PUT 'EM ON THE LIST;
AND THEY'LL NONE OF 'EM BE MISSED—
THEY'LL NONE OF 'EM BE MISSED!

[*Enter Pooh-Bah.*]

KO-KO. Pooh-Bah, it seems that the festivities in connection with my approaching marriage must last a week. I should like to do it handsomely, and I want to consult you as to the amount I ought to spend upon them.

POOH-BAH. Certainly. In which of my capacities? Chief Financial Officer, Head Legal Counsel, Head of Security, Keeper of the Key to the Executive Washroom?

KO-KO. Yes, suppose we say as Keeper of the Key to the Executive Washroom.

POOH-BAH. Speaking as Keeper of the Key to the Executive Washroom, I should say that, as the company will be paying for it, don't stint yourself, do it well.

KO-KO. Exactly--as the company will have to pay for it. That is your advice.

POOH-BAH. As Keeper of the Key to the Executive Washroom. Of course you will understand that, as Chief Financial Officer, I am bound to see that due economy is observed.

KO-KO. Oh! But you said just now "Don't stint yourself, do it well".

POOH-BAH. As Keeper of the Key to the Executive Washroom.

KO-KO. And now you say that due economy must be observed.

POOH-BAH. As Chief Financial Officer.

KO-KO. I see. Come over here, where the CFO can't hear us. *(They cross the stage.)* Now, as Head Legal Counsel, how do you advise me to deal with this difficulty?

POOH-BAH. Oh, as Head Legal Counsel, I should have no hesitation in saying "Chance it----"

KO-KO. Thank you. *(Shaking his hand.)* I will.

POOH-BAH. If it were not that, as Head of Security, I am bound to see that the rules aren't violated.

KO-KO. I see. Come over here where the Head of Security can't hear us. *(They cross the stage.)* Now, then, as OSHA Compliance Officer?

POOH-BAH. Of course, as OSHA Compliance Officer, I could propose suspending all the rules, if it were not that, as Head of Security, it would be my duty to resist it, tooth and nail. Or, as Payroll Supervisor, I could so cook the accounts that, as Chief Auditor, I should never discover the fraud. But then, as Chair of the Ethics Committee, it would be my duty to denounce my dishonesty and give myself into my own custody as Head of Security.

KO-KO. That's extremely awkward.

POOH-BAH. I don't say that all these distinguished people couldn't be squared; but it is right to tell you that they wouldn't be sufficiently degraded in their own estimation unless they were insulted with a very considerable bribe.

KO-KO. The matter shall have my careful consideration. But my bride and her co-workers approach, and any little compliment on your part, such as an abject grovel in a characteristic Japanese attitude, would be esteemed a favor.

POOH-BAH. No money, no grovel!

[*Exit together. Enter procession of Yum-Yum's co-workers, carrying file folders that fan out, heralding Yum-Yum, Peep-Bo, and Pitti-Sing.*]

CHORUS OF GIRLS.

COMES A TRAIN OF LITTLE LADIES
FROM WORDPERFECT TRAMMELS FREE,
EACH A LITTLE BIT AFRAID IS,
WONDERING WHAT THE NIGHT WILL BE!

IS IT BUT A WORLD OF TROUBLE--
SADNESS SET TO SONG?
IS ITS BEAUTY BUT A BUBBLE
BOUND TO BREAK ERE LONG?

ARE ITS PALACES AND PLEASURES
FANTASIES THAT FADE?
AND THE GLORY OF ITS TREASURES
SHADOW OF A SHADE?

SECRETARIES TWENTY UNDER,
FROM WORDPERFECT TRAMMELS FREE,
AND WE WONDER--HOW WE WONDER!--
WHAT ON EARTH THE NIGHT WILL BE!

TRIO. YUM-YUM, PEEP-BO, AND PITTI-SING, WITH CHORUS OF GIRLS.

THE THREE. THREE LITTLE MAIDS FROM TH'POOL ARE WE,
PERT AS A POOL-GIRL WELL CAN BE,
FILLED TO THE BRIM WITH GIRLISH GLEE,
THREE LITTLE MAIDS FROM TH'POOL!

YUM-YUM. EVERYTHING IS A SOURCE OF FUN. (*Chuckle.*)
PEEP-BO. NOBODY'S SAFE, FOR WE CARE FOR NONE! (*Chuckle.*)
PITTI-SING. LIFE IS A JOKE THAT'S JUST BEGUN! (*Chuckle.*)
THE THREE. THREE LITTLE MAIDS FROM TH'POOL!
ALL (*dancing*). THREE LITTLE MAIDS WHO, ALL UNWARY,
WORK AS A BUSY SECRETARY,
FREED FROM ITS TEDIUM – NOT SO MERRY
THE THREE (*suddenly demure*). THREE LITTLE MAIDS FROM TH'POOL!
YUM-YUM. ONE LITTLE MAID IS A BRIDE, YUM-YUM--
PEEP-BO. TWO LITTLE MAIDS IN ATTENDANCE COME--
PITTI-SING. THREE LITTLE MAIDS IS THE TOTAL SUM.
THE THREE. THREE LITTLE MAIDS FROM TH'POOL!
YUM-YUM. FROM THREE LITTLE MAIDS TAKE ONE AWAY.
PEEP-BO. TWO LITTLE MAIDS REMAIN, AND THEY--
PITTI-SING. WON'T HAVE TO WAIT VERY LONG, THEY SAY--
THE THREE. THREE LITTLE MAIDS FROM TH'POOL!
ALL (*dancing*). THREE LITTLE MAIDS WHO, ALL UNWARY,
WORK AS A BUSY SECRETARY,
FREED FROM ITS TEDIUM – NOT SO MERRY
THE THREE (*suddenly demure*). THREE LITTLE MAIDS FROM TH'POOL!

[*Enter Ko-Ko and Pooh-Bah.*]

KO-KO. At last, my bride that is to be! (*About to embrace her.*)

YUM-YUM. You're not going to kiss me before all these people?

KO-KO. Well, that was the idea.

YUM-YUM (*aside to Peep-Bo*). It seems odd, doesn't it?

PEEP-BO. It's rather peculiar.

PITTI-SING. Oh, I expect it's all right. Must have a beginning, you know.

YUM-YUM. Well, of course I know nothing about these things; but I've no objection if it's usual.

KO-KO. Oh, it's quite usual, I think. Eh, Chair of the Ethics Committee? (*Appealing to Pooh-Bah.*)

POOH-BAH. I have known it done. (*Ko-Ko embraces her.*)

YUM-YUM. Thank goodness that's over! (*Sees Nanki-Poo, and rushes to him.*) Why, that's never you? (*The three Girls rush to him and shake his hands, all speaking at once.*)

YUM-YUM. Oh, I'm so glad! I haven't seen you for ever so long, and I'm right at the top of the pool, and I've got three raises, and I've quit for good, and I'm not going back any more!

PEEP-BO. And have you got an engagement?--Yum-Yum's got one, but she doesn't like it, and she'd ever so much rather it was you! I've quit for good, and I'm not going back any more!

PITTI-SING. Now tell us all the news, because you go about everywhere, and we've been stuck in the secretarial pool, but, thank goodness, that's all over now, and we've quit for good, and we're not going back any more!

(*These three speeches are spoken together in one breath.*)

KO-KO. I beg your pardon. Will you present me?

YUM-YUM. Oh, this is the mail boy who used--

PEEP-BO. Oh, this is the sexy mailboy-who used--

PITTI-SING. Oh, it is only Nanki-Poo who used--

KO-KO. One at a time, if you please.

YUM-YUM. Oh, if you please he's the mailboy who used to play so beautifully on the--on the--

PITTI-SING. On the accordion.

YUM-YUM. Yes, I think that was the name of the instrument.

NANKI-POO. Sir, I have the misfortune to love your secretary, Yum-Yum--oh, I know I deserve your anger!

KO-KO. Anger! not a bit, my boy. Why, I love her myself. Charming little girl, isn't she? Pretty eyes, nice hair. Taking little thing, altogether. Very glad to hear my opinion backed by a competent authority. Thank you very much. Good-bye. (*To Pish-Tush.*) Take him away. (*Pish-Tush removes him.*)

PITTI-SING (*who has been examining Pooh-Bah*). I beg your pardon, but what is this? Competitor come to try a hostile take-over?

KO-KO. That is a Tremendous Swell.

PITTI-SING. Oh, it's alive. (*She starts back in alarm.*)

POOH-BAH. Go away, little girls. Can't talk to little girls like you. Go away, there's dears.

KO-KO. Allow me to present you, Pooh-Bah. These are my three secretaries. The one in the middle is my bride to be.

POOH-BAH. What do you want me to do? Mind, I will not kiss them.

KO-KO. No, no, you shan't kiss them; a little bow--a mere nothing--you needn't mean it, you know.

POOH-BAH. It goes against company policy. Rule #1, you know!

KO-KO. Come, come, make an effort, there's a good Vice President.

POOH-BAH. (*aside to Ko-Ko*). Well, I won't mean anything by it. (*with a great effort.*) How de do, little girls, how de do? (*Aside.*) Oh, my MBA!

KO-KO. That's very good. (*Girls indulge in suppressed laughter.*)

POOH-BAH. I see nothing to laugh at. It is very painful to me to have to say "How de do, little girls, how de do?" to secretaries. I'm not in the habit of saying "How de do, little girls, how de do?" to anybody under the rank of a Senior Project Manager.

KO-KO. (*aside to girls*). Don't laugh at him, he can't help it--he's under treatment for it. (*Aside to Pooh-Bah.*) Never mind them, they don't understand the loftiness of your position.

POOH-BAH. We know how lofty it is, don't we?

KO-KO. I should think we did! How an MBA of your importance can do it at all is a thing I never can, never shall understand.

[*Ko-Ko retires and goes off.*]

QUARTET AND CHORUS OF GIRLS. YUM-YUM, PEEP-BO, PITTI-SING, POOH-BAH.

YUM-YUM, PEEP-BO. So please you, Sir, we much regret
and PITTI-SING. If we have failed in etiquette
Towards a man of rank so high--
We shall know better by and by.
YUM-YUM. But youth, of course, must have its fling,
So pardon us,
So pardon us,
PITTI-SING. And don't, in girlhood's happy spring,
Be hard on us,
Be hard on us,
If we're inclined to dance and sing.
Tra la la, etc. *(Dancing.)*
CHORUS OF GIRLS. But youth, of course, etc.
POOH-BAH. I think you ought to recollect
You cannot show too much respect
Towards the highly titled few;
But nobody does, and why should you?
That youth at us should have its fling,
Is hard on us,
Is hard on us;
To our prerogative we cling--
So pardon us,
So pardon us,
If we decline to dance and sing.
Tra la la, etc. *(Dancing.)*

CHORUS OF GIRLS.. But youth, of course, must have its fling, etc.

[*Exit all but Yum-Yum. Enter Nanki-Poo.*]

NANKI-POO. Yum-Yum, at last we are alone! I have sought you night and day for three weeks, in the belief that your boss was fired, and I find that you are about to be married to him this afternoon!

YUM-YUM. Alas, yes!

NANKI-POO. But you do not love him?

YUM-YUM. Alas, no!

NANKI-POO. (*Aside*) Modified rapture! But why do you not refuse him?

YUM-YUM. What good would that do? He's my boss, and he wouldn't let me marry you! Besides—an IPS delivery man, who plays an accordion outside the secretarial pool is hardly a fitting husband for the Personal Assistant to the Vice President of Human Resources.

NANKI-POO. But---- (*Aside.*) Shall I tell her? Yes! She will not betray me! (*Aloud.*) What if it should prove that, after all, I am no delivery man?

YUM-YUM. There! I was certain of it, directly I saw you work!

NANKI-POO. What if it should prove that I am no other than the son of the CEO of Mikado Enterprises LLC.?

YUM-YUM. The son of the CEO of Mikado Enterprises LLC.! But why are you disguised as a mail boy turned IPS delivery man who plays the accordion? And what did you do to get fired? And will you promise never to do it again?

NANKI-POO. Some years ago I had the misfortune to captivate Katisha, the old cleaning lady who works nights in the offices. She misconstrued my customary affability into expressions of affection, and claimed to everyone that would hear that we *had* to get married. My father, the Lucius Junius Brutus of his race, ordered me to marry her within a week, or be fired and written out of the will. That night I cleaned out my locker and left Mikado Enterprises LLC., and, took the job of delivery driver for IPS, I returned bearing packages, which is how you found me – serenading you between expedited deliveries! (*Approaching her.*)

YUM-YUM. (*retreating*). If you please, I think you had better not come too near. The rules against flirting are excessively severe.

NANKI-POO. But we are quite alone, and nobody can see us.

YUM-YUM. Still, that don't make it right. To flirt is capital.

NANKI-POO. It is capital!

YUM-YUM. And we must obey rule #1.

NANKI-POO. What is rule #1?

YUM-YUM. No sexual touching – it's in the handbook.

NANKI-POO. If it were not for that, how happy we might be!

YUM-YUM. Happy indeed!

NANKI-POO. If it were not for rule #1, we should now be sitting side by side, like that. (*Sits by her.*)

YUM-YUM. Instead of being obliged to sit half a mile off, like that. (*Moves by a foot.*)

NANKI-POO. We should be gazing into each other's eyes, like that. (*Gazing at her sentimentally.*)

YUM-YUM. Breathing sighs of unutterable love--like that. (*Sighing and gazing lovingly at him.*)

NANKI-POO. With our arms round each other's waists, like that. (*Embracing her.*)

YUM-YUM. Yes, if it wasn't for rule #1.

NANKI-POO. If it wasn't for rule #1.

YUM-YUM. As it is, of course we couldn't do anything of the kind.

NANKI-POO. Not for worlds!

YUM-YUM. Being engaged to Ko-Ko, you know!

NANKI-POO. Being engaged to Ko-Ko!

DUET--YUM-YUM and NANKI-POO.

NANKI-POO. WERE YOU NOT TO KO-KO PLIGHTED,
I WOULD SAY IN TENDER TONE,
"LOVED ONE, LET US BE UNITED--
LET US BE EACH OTHER'S OWN!"

I WOULD MERGE ALL RANK AND STATION,
WORLDLY SNEERS ARE NOUGHT TO US,
AND, TO MARK MY ADMIRATION,
I WOULD KISS YOU FONDLY THUS-- (*Kisses her.*)
BOTH. I/HE WOULD KISS YOU/ME FONDLY THUS-- (*Kiss.*)
YUM-YUM. BUT AS I'M ENGAGED TO KO-KO,
TO EMBRACE YOU THUS, CON FUOCO,
WOULD DISTINCTLY BE NO GIUOCO,
AND FOR YAM I SHOULD GET TOKO--
BOTH. TOKO, TOKO, TOKO, TOKO!
NANKI-POO. SO, IN SPITE OF ALL TEMPTATION,
SUCH A THEME I'LL NOT DISCUSS,
AND ON NO CONSIDERATION
WILL I KISS YOU FONDLY THUS-- (*Kissing her.*)
LET ME MAKE IT CLEAR TO YOU,
THIS IS WHAT I'LL NEVER DO!
THIS, OH, THIS, OH, THIS, OH, THIS,--(*Kissing her.*)
TOGETHER. THIS, OH, THIS, ETC.

[*Exit in opposite directions. Enter Ko-Ko.*]

KO-KO. (*looking after Yum-Yum*). There she goes! To think how entirely my future happiness is wrapped up in that little parcel! Really, it hardly seems worth while! Oh, matrimony!-- (*Enter Pooh-Bah and Pish-Tush.*) Now then, what is it? Can't you see I'm soliloquizing? You have interrupted an apostrophe, sir!

PISH-TUSH. I am the bearer of a letter from the CEO of Mikado Enterprises...

TOGETHER. “L.L.C.”

KO-KO. (*taking it reverentially*). A letter from the CEO of Mikado Enterprises LLC.! What in the world can he have to say to me? (*Reads letter.*) Ah, here it is at last! I thought it would come sooner or later! The CEO of Mikado Enterprises LLC. is struck by the fact that no terminations have taken place here for a year, and decrees that unless somebody is fired without severance within one month the post of VP-Human Resources shall be abolished, and the Board reduced to the rank of a window washers!

PISH-TUSH. But that will involve us all in irretrievable ruin!

KO-KO. Yes. There is no help for it, I shall have to terminate somebody at once. The only question is, who shall it be?

POOH-BAH. Well, it seems unkind to say so, but as you're already on probation for flirting, everything seems to point to you.

KO-KO. To me? What are you talking about? I can't terminate myself.

POOH-BAH. Why not?

KO-KO. Why not? Because, in the first place, self termination is an extremely difficult, not to say dangerous, thing to attempt; and, in the second, it's self-centered, and to be self-centered is a capital offense.

POOH-BAH. That is so, no doubt.

PISH-TUSH. We could dispute that point.

POOH-BAH. True, it could be argued in six months, before the full Board.

KO-KO. Besides, I don't see how a man can yell at himself that he is fired and hand over his keys immediately to himself before being removed from the building.

POOH-BAH. A man might try.

PISH-TUSH. Even if you just yelled at yourself, that would be something.

POOH-BAH. It would be taken as an earnest of your desire to comply with the Company will.

KO-KO. No. Pardon me, but there I am adamant. As VP-Human Resources, my reputation is at stake, and I can't consent to embark on a professional operation unless I see my way to a successful result.

POOH-BAH. This professional conscientiousness is highly creditable to you, but it places us in a very awkward position.

KO-KO. My good sir, the awkwardness of your position is grace itself compared with that of a man engaged in the act of firing himself.

PISH-TUSH. I am afraid that, unless you can obtain a substitute ----

KO-KO. A substitute? Oh, certainly--nothing easier. (*To Pooh-Bah.*) Pooh-Bah, I appoint you Deputy VP-Human Resources.

POOH-BAH. I should be delighted. Such an appointment would realize my fondest dreams. But no, at any sacrifice, I must set bounds to my insatiable ambition!

<u>TRIO</u>
KO-KO

MY BRAIN IT TEAMS WITH ENDLESS SCHEMES
BOTH GOOD AND NEW FOR TITIPU;
BUT IF I FLIT, THE BENEFIT
THAT I'D DIFFUSE THE PLACE WOULD LOSE!
NOW EVERY MAN TO AID HIS CLAN
SHOULD PLOT AND PLAN AS BEST HE CAN,
AND SO, ALTHOUGH I'M READY TO GO,
YET RECOLLECT 'TWERE DISRESPECT
DID I NEGLECT TO THUS EFFECT
THIS AIM DIRECT, SO I OBJECT--
SO I OBJECT-- SO I OBJECT--

POOH-BAH

I AM SO PROUD, IF I ALLOWED
MY FAMILY PRIDE TO BE MY GUIDE,
I'D VOLUNTEER TO QUIT THIS HERE
INSTEAD OF YOU IN A MINUTE OR TWO,
BUT FAMILY PRIDE MUST BE DENIED,
AND SET ASIDE, AND MORTIFIED.
AND SO, ALTHOUGH I WISH TO GO,
AND GREATLY PINE TO BRIGHTLY SHINE,
AND TAKE THE LINE OF A HERO FINE,

WITH GRIEF CONDIGN I MUST DECLINE--
I MUST DECLINE-- I MUST DECLINE--

PISH-TUSH
I HEARD ONE DAY A GENTLEMAN SAY
VICE PRESIDENTS WHO ARE FIRED TOO
MAY SOON FIND WORK WITH OTHER JERKS,
AND SO THEY GO LIKE EBB AND FLOW.
IF THIS IS TRUE, IT'S JOLLY FOR YOU;
YOUR COURAGE SCREW TO BID US ADIEU,
AND GO AND SHOW BOTH FRIEND AND FOE
HOW MUCH YOU DARE. I'M QUITE AWARE
IT'S YOUR AFFAIR, YET I DECLARE
I'D TAKE YOUR SHARE, BUT I DON'T MUCH CARE--
I DON'T MUCH CARE-- I DON'T MUCH CARE--

ALL. TO SIT IN SOLEMN SILENCE IN A DULL, DARK SPACE,
IN A PESTILENTIAL CUBICLE, WITH A GREAT-LONG FACE,
AWAITING THE SENSATION OF THE OLD RAT RACE,
IT WOULD MAKE ME WANT TO DISAPPEAR WITHOUT A TRACE!

[*Exit Pooh. and Pish.*]

KO-KO. This is simply appalling! I, who commuted my own termination in favor of probation under pressure, simply in order to adhere to Rule #1, am now required to be fired within a month, and that by a man whom I have loaded with honors! Is this public gratitude? Is this--- (*Enter Nanki-Poo, with a trash basket and a shredder in his hands.*) Go away, sir! How dare you? Am I never to be permitted to soliloquize?

NANKI-POO. Oh, go on--don't mind me.

KO-KO. What are you going to do with that shredder?

NANKI-POO. I am about to terminate my unendurable existence.

KO-KO. *Terminate* your existence? Oh, nonsense! What for?

NANKI-POO. Because you are going to marry the girl I adore.

KO-KO. Nonsense, sir. I won't permit it. I am a humane man, and if you attempt anything of the kind I shall order your instant arrest. Come, sir, desist at once or I summon security.

NANKI-POO. That's absurd. If you attempt to call security, I instantly will jump out the window and fall to the street 33 floors below. (*They look out the window and down*)

KO-KO. No, no, don't do that. This is horrible! (*Suddenly.*) Why, you cold-blooded scoundrel, are you aware that, in taking your life, you are committing a crime which--which--which is against Rule # … *Oh!* (*Struck by an idea.*) Substitute!

NANKI-POO. What's the matter?

KO-KO. Is it absolutely certain that you are resolved to die?

NANKI-POO. Absolutely!

KO-KO. Will nothing shake your resolution?

NANKI-POO. Nothing.

KO-KO. Threats, entreaties, prayers--all useless?

NANKI-POO. All! My mind is made up.

KO-KO. Then, if you really mean what you say, and if you are absolutely resolved to die, and if nothing whatever will shake your determination--don't spoil yourself by committing suicide, but let me hire you as mailboy or something and then terminate you first!

NANKI-POO. I don't see how that would benefit me.

KO-KO. You don't? Observe: you'll have a month to live, and you'll get paid like a Vice President - at my expense. When the day comes there'll be a grand public hearing -- you'll be the central figure--no one will attempt to deprive you of that distinction. There'll be a meeting--witnesses--memos—intercoms abuzz everywhere--all the girls in tears--Yum-Yum distracted--then, when it's all over, general rejoicings, and free hors d'oevres in the executive dining room. You won't be able to have any, but they'll be there all the same.

NANKI-POO. Do you think Yum-Yum would really be distracted at my termination?

KO-KO. I am convinced of it. Bless you, she's the most tender-hearted little creature alive.

NANKI-POO. I should be sorry to cause her pain. Perhaps, after all, if I were to withdraw from Japan, and travel in Europe for a couple of years, I might contrive to forget her.

KO-KO. Oh, I don't think you could forget Yum-Yum so easily; and, after all, what is more miserable than a love-blighted life?

NANKI-POO. True.

KO-KO. Life without Yum-Yum--why, it seems absurd!

NANKI-POO. And yet there are a good many people in the world who have to endure it.

KO-KO. Poor devils, yes! You are quite right not to be of their number.

NANKI-POO. (*suddenly*). I won't be of their number!

KO-KO. Noble fellow!

NANKI-POO. I'll tell you how we'll manage it. Let me marry Yum-Yum to-morrow, and in a month you may terminate me, and I'll make her a widow all at the same time!

KO-KO. No, no. I draw the line at Yum-Yum.

NANKI-POO. Very good. If you can draw the line, so can I. (*Putting shredder in the basket.*)

KO-KO. Stop, stop--listen one moment--be reasonable. How can I consent to your marrying Yum-Yum if I'm going to marry her myself?

NANKI-POO. My good friend, she'll be a widow in a month, and you can marry her then.

KO-KO. That's true, of course. I quite see that. But, dear me! my position during the next month will be most unpleasant--most unpleasant.

NANKI-POO. Not half so unpleasant as my position at the end of it. (*makes hands like shredder*)

KO-KO. But--dear me!--well--I agree--after all, it's only putting off my wedding for a month. But you won't prejudice her against me, will you? You see, I've educated her to be my wife;

she's been taught to regard me as a wise and good man. Now I shouldn't like her views on that point disturbed.

NANKI-POO. Trust me, she shall never learn the truth from me.

KO-KO. Just sign right here…and here… and here… and here….Welcome to Mikado Enterprises, L.L.C.

ACT 1 FINALE.

[*Enter Chorus, Pooh-Bah, and Pish-Tush.*]

CHORUS. WITH ASPECT STERN
AND GLOOMY STRIDE,
WE COME TO LEARN
HOW YOU DECIDE.

DON'T HESITATE
YOUR CHOICE TO NAME,
A DREADFUL FATE
YOU'LL SUFFER ALL THE SAME.

POOH-BAH. TO ASK YOU WHAT YOU MEAN TO DO WE PUNCTUALLY APPEAR.

KO-KO. CONGRATULATE ME, GENTLEMEN, I'VE FOUND A VOLUNTEER!

ALL. THE JAPANESE EQUIVALENT FOR HEAR, HEAR, HEAR!

KO-KO. (*presenting him*). 'TIS NANKI-POO!

ALL. HAIL, NANKI-POO!

KO-KO. I THINK HE'LL DO?

ALL. YES, YES, HE'LL DO!

KO-KO. HE YIELDS HIS JOB IF I'LL YUM-YUM SURRENDER.
NOW I ADORE THAT GIRL WITH PASSION TENDER,
AND COULD NOT YIELD HER WITH A READY WILL,
OR HER ALLOT, IF I DID NOT
ADORE MYSELF WITH PASSION TENDERER STILL!

[*Enter Yum-Yum, Peep-Bo, and Pitti-Sing.*]

ALL. AH, YES! HE LOVES HIMSELF WITH PASSION TENDERER STILL!

KO-KO. (*to Nanki-Poo*). TAKE HER--SHE'S YOURS!

[*Exit Ko-Ko*]

ENSEMBLE AND PRINCIPLES.

NANKI-POO. THE THREATENED CLOUD HAS PASSED AWAY,
YUM-YUM. AND BRIGHTLY SHINES THE DAWNING DAY;
NANKI-POO. WHAT THOUGH THE NIGHT MAY COME TOO SOON,
YUM-YUM. THERE'S YET A MONTH OF AFTERNOON!

NANKI-POO, POOH-BAH, YUM-YUM, PITTI-SING, AND PEEP-BO.

THEN LET THE THRONG
OUR JOY ADVANCE,
WITH LAUGHING SONG
AND MERRY DANCE,

CHORUS. WITH JOYOUS SHOUT AND RINGING CHEER,
INAUGURATE OUR BRIEF CAREER!

PITTI-SING. A DAY, A WEEK, A MONTH, A YEAR--
YUM-YUM. OR FAR OR NEAR, OR FAR OR NEAR,
POOH-BAH. LIFE'S EVENTIME COMES MUCH TOO SOON,
PITTI-SING. YOU'LL LIVE AT LEAST A HONEYMOON!
ALL. THEN LET THE THRONG, ETC.
CHORUS. WITH JOYOUS SHOUT, ETC.

SOLO--POOH-BAH.

AS IN A MONTH YOU'VE GOT TO DIE,
IF KO-KO TELLS US TRUE,
'TWERE EMPTY COMPLIMENT TO CRY
"LONG LIFE TO NANKI-POO!"
BUT AS ONE MONTH YOU HAVE TO LIVE
AS FELLOW-CITIZEN,
THIS TOAST WITH THREE TIMES THREE WE'LL GIVE--
"LONG LIFE TO YOU--TILL THEN!"

[*Exit Pooh-Bah.*]

CHORUS. MAY ALL GOOD FORTUNE PROSPER YOU,
MAY YOU HAVE HEALTH AND RICHES TOO,
MAY YOU SUCCEED IN ALL YOU DO!
LONG LIFE TO YOU--TILL THEN!

[*Dance. Enter Katisha melodramatically, pushing a cleaning cart.*]

KATISHA. YOUR REVELS CEASE! ASSIST ME, ALL OF YOU!
CHORUS. WHY, WHO IS THIS WHOSE EVIL EYES
RAIN BLIGHT ON OUR FESTIVITIES?
KATISHA. I CLAIM MY PERJURED LOVER, NANKI-POO!
OH, FOOL! TO SHUN DELIGHTS THAT NEVER CLOY!
CHORUS. GO, LEAVE THY DEADLY WORK UNDONE!
KATISHA. COME BACK, OH, SHALLOW FOOL! COME BACK TO JOY!
CHORUS. AWAY, AWAY! ILL-FAVOURED ONE!
NANKI-POO. (*aside to Yum-Yum*). AH! 'TIS KATISHA!
THE MAID OF WHOM I TOLD YOU. *(About to go.)*
KATISHA. (*detaining him*). NO! YOU SHALL NOT GO,
THESE ARMS SHALL THUS ENFOLD YOU!
KATISHA. (*addressing Nanki-Poo*).
OH FOOL, THAT FLEEST
MY HALLOWED JOYS!
OH BLIND, THAT SEEST
NO EQUIPOISE!
OH RASH, THAT JUDGEST
FROM HALF, THE WHOLE!
OH BASE, THAT GRUDGEST
LOVE'S LIGHTEST DOLE!
THY HEART UNBIND,
OH FOOL, OH BLIND!
GIVE ME MY PLACE,
OH RASH, OH BASE!
CHORUS. IF SHE'S THY BRIDE, RESTORE HER PLACE,
OH FOOL, OH BLIND, OH RASH, OH BASE!
KATISHA. (*addressing Yum-Yum*).
PINK CHEEK, THAT RULEST
WHERE WISDOM SERVES!
BRIGHT EYE, THAT FOOLEST
HEROIC NERVES!
ROSE LIP, THAT SCORNEST
LORE-LADEN YEARS!
SMOOTH TONGUE, THAT WARNEST

WHO RIGHTLY HEARS!
THY DOOM IS NIGH.
PINK CHEEK, BRIGHT EYE!
THY KNELL IS RUNG,
ROSE LIP, SMOOTH TONGUE!

CHORUS. IF TRUE HER TALE, THY KNELL IS RUNG,
PINK CHEEK, BRIGHT EYE, ROSE LIP, SMOOTH TONGUE!

PITTI-SING. AWAY, NOR PROSECUTE YOUR QUEST--
FROM OUR INTENTION, WELL EXPRESSED,
YOU CANNOT TURN US!
THE STATE OF YOUR CONNUBIAL VIEWS
TOWARDS THE PERSON YOU ACCUSE
DOES NOT CONCERN US!
FOR HE'S GOING TO MARRY YUM-YUM--

ALL. YUM-YUM!

PITTI-SING. YOUR ANGER PRAY BURY,
FOR ALL WILL BE MERRY,
I THINK YOU HAD BETTER SUCCUMB--

ALL. COME--COME!

PITTI-SING. AND JOIN OUR EXPRESSIONS OF GLEE.
ON THIS SUBJECT I PRAY YOU BE DUMB--

ALL. DUMB--DUMB.

PITTI-SING. YOU'LL FIND THERE ARE MANY
WHO'LL WED FOR A PENNY--
THE WORD FOR YOUR GUIDANCE IS "MUM"--

ALL. MUM--MUM!

PITTI-SING. THERE'S LOTS OF GOOD FISH IN THE SEA!

ALL. ON THIS SUBJECT WE PRAY YOU BE DUMB, ETC.

SOLO--KATISHA.

THE HOUR OF GLADNESS
IS DEAD AND GONE;
IN SILENT SADNESS
I LIVE ALONE!
THE HOPE I CHERISHED

ALL LIFELESS LIES,
AND ALL HAS PERISHED
SAVE LOVE, WHICH NEVER DIES!
OH, FAITHLESS ONE, THIS INSULT YOU SHALL RUE!
IN VAIN FOR MERCY ON YOUR KNEES YOU'LL SUE.
I'LL TEAR THE MASK FROM YOUR DISGUISING!

NANKI-POO. (*aside*). NOW COMES THE BLOW!
KATISHA. PREPARE YOURSELVES FOR NEWS SURPRISING!
NANKI-POO. (*aside*). HOW FOIL MY FOE?
KATISHA. NO MAIL BOY HE, DESPITE BRAVADO!
YUM-YUM. (*aside, struck by an idea*). HA! HA! I KNOW!
KATISHA. HE IS THE SON OF YOUR----

(*Nanki-Poo, Yum-Yum, and Chorus, interrupting, sing Japanese words, to drown her voice.*)

NANKI-POO, YUM-YUM, AND CHORUS. O NI! BIKKURI SHAKKURI TO!
KATISHA. IN VAIN YOU INTERRUPT WITH THIS TORNADO!
HE IS THE ONLY SON OF YOUR----
ALL. O NI! BIKKURI SHAKKURI TO!
KATISHA. I'LL SPOIL----
ALL. O NI! BIKKURI SHAKKURI TO!
KATISHA. YOUR FUN PARTY-OH!
HE IS THE SON----
ALL. O NI! BIKKURI SHAKKURI TO!
KATISHA. OF YOUR----
ALL. O NI! BIKKURI SHAKKURI TO!
KATISHA. THE SON OF YOUR----
ALL. O NI! BIKKURI SHAKKURI TO! OYA! OYA!

KATISHA.
YE TORRENTS ROAR!
YE TEMPESTS HOWL!
YOUR WRATH OUTPOUR

WITH ANGRY GROWL!
DO YE YOUR WORST, MY VENGEANCE CALL
SHALL RISE TRIUMPHANT OVER ALL!
PREPARE FOR WOE,
YE HAUGHTY LORDS,
AT ONCE I GO
MIKADO-WARDS,
MY WRONGS WITH VENGEANCE SHALL
BE CROWNED!
MY WRONGS WITH VENGEANCE SHALL
BE CROWNED!

THE OTHERS.
WE'LL HEAR NO MORE,
ILL-OMENED OWL.
TO JOY WE SOAR,
DESPITE YOUR SCOWL!
THE ECHOES OF OUR FESTIVAL
SHALL RISE TRIUMPHANT OVER ALL!
AWAY YOU GO,
COLLECT YOUR HORDES;
PROCLAIM YOUR WOE
IN DISMAL CHORDS
WE DO NOT HEED THEIR DISMAL SOUND
FOR JOY REIGNS EVERYWHERE AROUND.

(*Katisha rushes furiously from the stage, riding her cleaning cart.*)

END OF ACT I.

ACT II

SCENE.—The women's bathroom of Mikado Enterprises, LLC.

[*Yum-Yum discovered seated, surrounded by maidens, who are finishing their coiffes as she fixes her hair and doing her make up, as she judges of the effect in a mirror. Yum-Yum may be blonde, in which case, "raven hair" becomes "maiden hair".*]

SOLO--PITTI-SING and CHORUS OF GIRLS.

CHORUS. BRAID THE RAVEN HAIR--
WEAVE THE SUPPLE TRESS--
DECK THE MAIDEN FAIR
IN HER LOVELINESS--
PAINT THE PRETTY FACE--
DYE THE CORAL LIP--
EMPHASIZE THE GRACE
OF HER LADYSHIP!
ART AND NATURE, THUS ALLIED,
GO TO MAKE A PRETTY BRIDE.

SOLO--PITTI-SING.

SIT WITH DOWNCAST EYE
LET IT BRIM WITH DEW--
TRY IF YOU CAN CRY--
WE WILL DO SO, TOO.
WHEN YOU'RE SUMMONED, START
LIKE A FRIGHTENED ROE--
FLUTTER, LITTLE HEART,
COLOR, COME AND GO!
MODESTY AT MARRIAGE-TIDE
WELL BECOMES A PRETTY BRIDE!

CHORUS. BRAID THE RAVEN HAIR, ETC.

[*Exit Pitti-Sing, Peep-Bo, and Chorus.*]

YUM-YUM. Yes, I am indeed beautiful! Sometimes I sit and wonder, in my artless Japanese way, why it is that I am so much more attractive than anybody else in the whole world. Can this be vanity? No! Nature is lovely and rejoices in her loveliness. I am a child of Nature, and take after my mother.

SONG--YUM-YUM.

THE SUN, WHOSE RAYS
ARE ALL ABLAZE
WITH EVER-LIVING GLORY,
DOES NOT DENY
HIS MAJESTY--
HE SCORNS TO TELL A STORY!
HE DON'T EXCLAIM,
"I BLUSH FOR SHAME,
SO KINDLY BE INDULGENT."
BUT, FIERCE AND BOLD,
IN FIERY GOLD,
HE GLORIES ALL EFFULGENT!
I MEAN TO RULE THE EARTH,
AS HE THE SKY--
WE REALLY KNOW OUR WORTH,
THE SUN AND I!
OBSERVE HIS FLAME,
THAT PLACID DAME,
THE MOON'S CELESTIAL HIGHNESS;
THERE'S NOT A TRACE
UPON HER FACE
OF DIFFIDENCE OR SHYNESS:
SHE BORROWS LIGHT
THAT, THROUGH THE NIGHT,
MANKIND MAY ALL ACCLAIM HER!
AND, TRUTH TO TELL,

SHE LIGHTS UP WELL,
SO I, FOR ONE, DON'T BLAME HER!
AH, PRAY MAKE NO MISTAKE,
WE ARE NOT SHY;
WE'RE VERY WIDE AWAKE,
THE MOON AND I!

[*Enter Pitti-Sing and Peep-Bo.*]

YUM-YUM. Yes, everything seems to smile upon me. I am to be married to-day to the man I love best and I believe I am the very happiest girl in Japan!

PEEP-BO. The happiest girl indeed, for she is indeed to be envied who has attained happiness even if . . .

YUM-YUM. even if . . . what?

PEEP-BO. Well, after all, your husband's plan is to put himself through the shredder [*all flip open their pda's to check the date*] one month from now. That's kind of a drawback, wouldn't you say?.

PITTI-SING. Well, I don't know . . . It all depends!

PEEP-BO. I'll bet Nanki-Poo will think it's a drawback!

PITTI-SING. [*Looks pointedly at Yum Yum*] Well….Not necessarily. It all depends!

YUM-YUM. (*in tears*). I think it's perfectly awful of you to bring up my husband's shredding on the very day of my wedding! If my married happiness is to be--to be--

PEEP-BO. Shredded? [*She makes her fingers like shredded paper*]

YUM-YUM. Well, shredded--in a month, why do you have to remind me? (*Weeping.*)

[*Enter Nanki-Poo with Security Guard*]

NANKI-POO. Yum-Yum in tears--and on her wedding morn!

YUM-YUM. (*sobbing*). They've been reminding me that in a month you're to be shredded! (*Bursts into tears.*)

PITTI-SING. Yes, we've been reminding her that you're to be shredded. (*Bursts into tears.*)

PEEP-BO. It's quite true, you know, you are to be shredded! (*Bursts into tears.*)

NANKI-POO. (*aside*). Humph! Now, *some* bridegrooms would be depressed by this sort of thing! (*Aloud.*) A month? Well, what's a month? Hah! These divisions of time are purely arbitrary. Who says twenty-four hours make a day?

PITTI-SING. It's a rumor going around.

NANKI-POO. Then we'll change it. We'll call each second a minute--each minute an hour--each hour a day--and each day a year. At that rate we've about thirty years of married happiness next month. Old people know what I'm talking about!

PEEP-BO. And, at that rate, the second act is already four hours and three-quarters long! [*Exit Peep-Bo.*]

YUM-YUM. Wow! What a bargain for only $10!

NANKI-POO. That's the way to look at it! Don't be downhearted! There's a silver lining to every cloud.

YUM-YUM. Certainly. Let's--let's be perfectly happy! (*Almost in tears.*)

SECURITY GUARD. By all means. Let's--let's thoroughly enjoy ourselves.

PITTI-SING. It's--it's foolish to cry! (*Trying to force a laugh.*)

YUM-YUM. Quite ridiculous! (*Trying to laugh.*)

(*All break into a forced and melancholy laugh.*)

MADRIGAL.--YUM-YUM, PITTI-SING, NANKI-POO, and SECURITY GUARD

GUARD

BRIGHTLY DAWNS OUR WEDDING DAY;
JOYOUS HOUR, WE GIVE THEE GREETING!
WHITHER, WHITHER ART THOU FLEETING?
FICKLE MOMENT, PRITHEE STAY!
WHAT THOUGH MORTAL JOYS BE HOLLOW?
PLEASURES COME, IF SORROWS FOLLOW:

THOUGH THE TOLLING SOUND, ERE LONG,
DING DONG! DING DONG!
YET UNTIL THE SHADOWS FALL
OVER ONE AND OVER ALL,
SING A MERRY MADRIGAL--
A MADRIGAL!
FAL-LA--FAL-LA! ETC. (*Ending in tears.*)

LET US DRY THE READY TEAR,
THOUGH THE HOURS ARE SURELY CREEPING
LITTLE NEED FOR WOEFUL WEEPING,
TILL THE SAD SUNDOWN IS NEAR.
ALL MUST SIP THE CUP OF SORROW--
I TO-DAY AND THOU TO-MORROW;
THIS THE CLOSE OF EVERY SONG--
DING DONG! DING DONG!
WHAT, THOUGH SOLEMN SHADOWS FALL,
SOONER, LATER, OVER ALL?
SING A MERRY MADRIGAL--
A MADRIGAL!
FAL-LA--FAL-LA! ETC. (*Ending in tears.*)

[*Exit Pitti-Sing and Security Guard. Nanki-Poo embraces Yum-Yum. Enter Ko-Ko. Nanki-Poo releases Yum-Yum.*]

KO-KO. Go on--don't mind me.

NANKI-POO. I'm afraid we're upsetting you.

KO-KO. Never mind, I have to get used to it. Only please do it by degrees. Begin by putting your arm round her waist. (*Nanki-Poo does so.*) There; let me get used to that first.

YUM-YUM. Oh, wouldn't you like to sneak off somewhere? It must pain you to see us so affectionate together!

KO-KO. No, I have to get used to it! Now let her head to rest on your shoulder.

NANKI-POO. Like that? (*He does so. Ko-Ko much affected.*)

KO-KO. Yes - now--kiss her! (*He does so. Ko-Ko writhes with anguish.*) Oh - it's simple torture!

YUM-YUM. Come on, cheer up. After all, it's only for a month.

KO-KO. No. It's no use deluding myself with false hopes.

NANKI-POO. and YUM. What do you mean?

KO-KO. (*to Yum-Yum*). My child--my poor child! (*Aside.*) How shall I break it to her? (*Aloud.*) My little bride that was to have been?

YUM-YUM. (*delighted*). *Was* to have been?

KO-KO. Yes, you never *can* be mine now!

NANKI-POO. and YUM-YUM. (*simultaneously, in ecstacy*) What! Yess!

KO-KO. I just found out that in the Mikado Enterprises, LLC Discipline Policy Manual, Chapter 13, Section 4, Paragraph 12.5, that when an employee is shredded his wife, if also employed, is to be drowned in a vat of White-Out®.

NANKI-POO. and YUM-YUM. Drowned in a vat of White-Out®!

KO-KO. Drowned in a vat of White-Out®. It's a most unpleasant termination.

NANKI-POO. But where did you hear about that policy?

KO-KO. Oh, from Pooh-Bah. He's the Chief Legal Counsel.

YUM-YUM. But he may be misinterpreting the policy!

KO-KO. So I thought; so I consulted the Head of Security, Keeper of the Key to the Executive Washroom, Refiller of the Lobby Candy Machine, OSHA Compliance Officer, Chaplain to the Board, and Principal of Wareham High School. They're all of the same opinion. Never knew such unanimity on a point of policy in my life!

NANKI-POO. But wait! This policy has never been enforced!

KO-KO. Not yet. You see, flirting is the only violation punishable with shredding, and married men never flirt.

NANKI-POO. Of course, they don't. I quite forgot that! Well, I suppose my dream of happiness is over!

YUM-YUM. Darling--I don't want to appear selfish, and I love you with all my heart--I don't suppose I will ever love anybody else half as much--but when I agreed to marry you--my pet--I had no idea--pet--that I would have to be drowned in White-Out® in a month!

NANKI-POO. Me neither! It's the first time I ever heard of it!

YUM-YUM. It--it makes a difference, doesn't it?

NANKI-POO. It does make a difference, of course.

YUM-YUM. You see—white out--it's such a . . . *pale* death!

NANKI-POO. Talk about the ultimate correction fluid!

YUM-YUM. You see my *problem*, don't you?

NANKI-POO. Yes, and I see *my* problem. If I insist that you carry out your promise, I doom you to a hideous death; if I release you, then you have to marry Ko-Ko right away!

TRIO.--YUM-YUM, NANKI-POO, and KO-KO.

YUM-YUM. HERE'S A HOW-DE-DO!
IF I MARRY YOU,
WHEN YOUR TIME HAS COME TO PERISH,
THEN THE MAIDEN WHOM YOU CHERISH
MUST BE WHITENED, TOO!
HERE'S A HOW-DE-DO!

NANKI-POO. HERE'S A PRETTY MESS!
IN A MONTH, OR LESS,
I MUST DIE WITHOUT A WEDDING!
LET THE BITTER TEARS I'M SHEDDING
WITNESS MY DISTRESS,
HERE'S A PRETTY MESS!

KO-KO. HERE'S A STATE OF THINGS
TO HER LIFE SHE CLINGS!
MATRIMONIAL DEVOTION

DOESN'T SEEM TO SUIT HER NOTION--
WHITE- OUT® DEATH IT BRINGS!
HERE'S A STATE OF THINGS!

ENSEMBLE-- YUM-YUM AND NANKI-POO.
YUM-YUM AND NANKI-POO.
WITH A PASSION THAT'S INTENSE
I WORSHIP AND ADORE,
BUT THE LAWS OF COMMON SENSE
WE OUGHTN'T TO IGNORE.
IF WHAT HE SAYS IS TRUE,
'TIS DEATH TO MARRY YOU!
HERE'S A PRETTY STATE OF THINGS!
HERE'S A PRETTY HOW-DE-DO!
KO-KO.
WITH A PASSION THAT'S INTENSE
YOU WORSHIP AND ADORE,
BUT THE LAWS OF COMMON SENSE
YOU OUGHTN'T TO IGNORE.
IF WHAT I SAY IS TRUE,
'TIS DEATH TO MARRY YOU!
HERE'S A PRETTY STATE OF THINGS!
HERE'S A PRETTY HOW-DE-DO!

[*Exit Yum-Yum.*]

KO-KO. (*going up to Nanki-Poo*). My poor boy, I'm really very sorry for you.

NANKI-POO. Thanks. I'm sure you are.

KO-KO. You see I'm quite helpless.

NANKI-POO. I quite see that.

KO-KO. I can't conceive anything more distressing than to have one's marriage broken off at the last moment. But you miss a wedding--you can come to mine!

NANKI-POO. That's good of you, but that's impossible.

KO-KO. Why so?

NANKI-POO. To-day I shred myself.

KO-KO. What do you mean?

NANKI-POO. I can't live without Yum-Yum. This afternoon, "zhzhzhzhzhzhzhzh" [*makes fingers go like shredder*].

KO-KO. No, no--pardon me--I can't allow that.

NANKI-POO. Why not?

KO-KO. Why, hang it all, you're under contract to be terminated by the Vice President of Human Resources after one month's Probationary period is up! If you shred yourself, what's to become of me? Why, I'll have to be terminated in your place!

NANKI-POO. Yep! Looks that way!

[*Enter Pooh-Bah.*]

KO-KO. Now then, Pooh-Bah, what is it?

POOH-BAH. The CEO of Mikado Enterprises, LLC. is on the way and will be here in ten minutes.

KO-KO. The CEO of Mikado Enterprises, LLC! … Must be coming to see whether the termination orders have been carried out! (*To Nanki-Poo.*) Now look here, you know—this is getting serious—a deal's a deal, and you really shouldn't frustrate the wheels of beaurocracy by committing suicide. As a man of honor and a gentleman, you are bound to let me terminate you.

NANKI-POO. Fine. Fire me.

KO-KO. What, now?

NANKI-POO. Yup. Right now.

POOH-BAH. Do it! Oh goody! Do it!!

KO-KO. My good sir, I can't just terminate you now. You have only been an employee for hours now. The Mikado Enterprises, LLC Discipline Policy Manual, Chapter 13, Section 6, Paragraph 2.1 says that an employee may not be terminated without first undergoing a 30 day probationary period.

POOH-BAH. Still, as Vice President of Human Resources --

--

KO-KO. My good sir, as Vice President of Human Resources, I've got to terminate him in a month. I t can't be done yet. I don't know how it's done. I'm going to study the manual. I'll start with Page 1 and work my way through to Page 476 if I have to to find a loophole! (*Weeps.*)

NANKI-POO. Come, my poor fellow, we all have unpleasant jobs at times; after all, what is it? If I don't mind, why should you? Remember, it has to be done sooner or later.

KO-KO. (*springing up suddenly*). It does? I'm not so sure about that!

NANKI-POO. What do you mean?

KO-KO. Why should I terminate you when making an affidavit that you've quit will do just as well? Here are plenty of witnesses--the Head of Security, Keeper of the Key to the Executive Washroom, Refiller of the Lobby Candy Machine, OSHA Compliance Officer, Chaplain to the Board, and Principal of Wareham High School.

NANKI-POO. But where are they?

KO-KO. There they are. They'll all swear to it--won't you? (*To Pooh-Bah.*)

POOH-BAH. Am I to understand that all of us high company officials are expected to perjure ourselves to ensure your job?

KO-KO. Why not! You'll be grossly insulted, as usual.

POOH-BAH. Will the insult be cash or credit?

KO-KO. It will be a Postal Money Order.

POOH-BAH. (*Aside.*) Well, that will come in handy. (*Aloud.*) Very good. Make something up, and I'll endorse it! (*Aside.*) Ha! ha! Family Pride, how do you like that, buddy?

NANKI-POO. But I tell you, life without Yum-Yum----

KO-KO. Oh, Yum-Yum, Yum-Yum! Forget Yum-Yum! Here, Mr. VP (*to Pooh-Bah*), go and fetch Yum-Yum. (*Exit Pooh-Bah.*) Take Yum-Yum. Marry Yum-Yum, only go away and never come back again. (*Enter Pooh-Bah with Yum-Yum.*) Here she is. Yum-Yum, are you particularly busy?

YUM-YUM. Not really, no..

KO-KO. You got five minutes to spare?

YUM-YUM. Yes.

KO-KO. Then go along with the Chaplain to the Board; he'll marry you at once.

YUM-YUM. But if I'm to be drowned in White-Out®…?

KO-KO. Now, don't ask any questions, just do as I tell you, and Nanki-Poo will explain all.

NANKI-POO. But wait----

KO-KO. Not a chance! Here comes the CEO, no doubt to ascertain whether I've obeyed the directive, and if you're still here he'll never believe me. (*Exit Nanki-Poo and Yum-Yum, followed by Pooh-Bah.*) Close thing that, for here he comes! [*Exit Ko-Ko.*]

[*Entrance of CEO with Katisha. The Company chorus accompanies his entrance.*]

CHORUS. MIYA SAMA, MIYA SAMA,
ON N'M-MA NO MAYE NI
PIRA-PIRA SURU NO WA
NAN GIA NA
TOKO TONYARE TONYARE NA?

DUET--CEO AND KATISHA.

CEO. IN EVERY TIME AND PLACE
OBEDIENCE I EXPECT;
I'M THE CHIEF EXEC OF THIS PLACE--

KATISHA. AND I'M HIS DAUGHTER-IN-LAW ELECT!
HE'LL MARRY HIS SON
(HE'S ONLY GOT ONE)
TO HIS DAUGHTER-IN-LAW ELECT!

CEO. MY MORALS HAVE BEEN DECLARED
PARTICULARLY CORRECT;

KATISHA. BUT THEY'RE NOTHING AT ALL, COMPARED
WITH THOSE OF HIS DAUGHTER-IN-LAW ELECT!
BOW--BOW--
TO HIS DAUGHTER-IN-LAW ELECT!

ALL. BOW--BOW-- TO HIS DAUGHTER-IN-LAW ELECT.

CEO. IN A FATHERLY KIND OF WAY
I MODEL WHAT I EXPECT,
ALL CHEERFULLY OWN MY SWAY--
KATISHA. EXCEPT HIS DAUGHTER-IN-LAW ELECT!
AS TOUGH AS A BONE,
WITH A WILL OF HER OWN,
IS HIS DAUGHTER-IN-LAW ELECT!
CEO. MY NATURE IS LOVE AND LIGHT--
MY FREEDOM FROM ALL DEFECT--
KATISHA. IS INSIGNIFICANT QUITE,
COMPARED WITH HIS DAUGHTER-IN-LAW ELECT!
BOW--BOW--
TO HIS DAUGHTER-IN-LAW ELECT!
ALL. BOW--BOW-- TO HIS DAUGHTER-IN-LAW ELECT!

[*Enter Pooh-Bah, Ko-Ko, and Pitti-Sing. All kowtow. Pooh-Bah hands a paper to Ko-Ko.*]

KO-KO. I am honored in being permitted to welcome you, CEO. I think I know why you are visiting today. The termination has taken place.

CEO. Oh, you've had a termination, have you?

KO-KO. Yes. The Supervisor of Payroll has just handed me this notice.

POOH-BAH. I am the Supervisor of Payroll. (*Ko-Ko hands certificate to the CEO.*)

CEO. And this is the certificate of his termination. (*Reads.*) "In the presence of the Head of Security, Keeper of the Key to the Executive Washroom, Refiller of the Lobby Candy Machine, OSHA Compliance Officer, Chaplain to the Board, and Principal of Wareham High School.----"

POOH-BAH. They were all present, Sir. I counted them myself.

CEO. Very good house. I wish I'd been in time for the performance.

KO-KO. A tough fellow he was, too--a man of gigantic self composure. His distress was terrific. It was a remarkable scene.

CEO. Describe it.

KO-KO. He actually cried, as we let him go. He was in a state of wild alarm-- With a frightful, frantic, fearful frown, I bared my teeth. I upbraided him with alacrity. He fell to his knees and he squirmed and pleaded. I drew forth my Waterman pen - Oh, I will never, never forget his cries, or the shriek that shrieked as I gnashed my teeth, when I grabbed from my desk, my Waterman pen!

PITTI-SING. He shivered and shook as he signed the slip for the firing he didn't deserve; When all of a sudden his eye met mine, And it seemed to brace his nerve; He nodded his head and wiped his brow and he whistled a song. as the pen signed the termination papers! When a man's afraid, a beautiful girl is an encouraging sight to see, and I'm so glad I could be there to help him out in his moment of extreme distress.

POOH-BAH. Now though you'd have thought he knew his life and future employability were hopeless, still, he smiled and bowed and thanked us for the opportunity to work here and hoped he might use us as a reference someday. He was as humble as could be; clearly recognizing a man of high standing. It was a touching sight to see. Though unemployed, he couldn't forget due deference to me!

SECURITY GUARD. He speaks the truth, It all took place exactly as he says! I took his keys and saw him out of the building. [*Exit.*]

CEO. All this is very interesting, and I should like to have seen it. But I came about a totally different matter. A year ago my son, the heir to the Chairmanship of the Board, bolted from our little company.

KO-KO. He did?! Did he have any reason to be dissatisfied with his position?

KATISHA. None whatever. On the contrary, I was going to marry him—and he *STILL* took off!

POOH-BAH. I am surprised that he would have run from someone so lovely!

KATISHA. That's not true.

POOH-BAH. No!

KATISHA. You say that I am not beautiful because my face is plain. But you know nothing; you are still unenlightened. Learn, then, that it is not in the face alone that beauty is to be found. My face *is* unattractive!

POOH-BAH. It sure *is*.

KATISHA. But I have a left shoulder-blade that will knock you out! People come miles to see it. My right elbow has it's own fan club.

POOH-BAH. Let's see!

KATISHA. It is only open on Mondays and Thursdays, with a ticket. In fact, I'm known all over the internet.

KO-KO. And he still ran away!

CEO. And is now working in this town, disguised as an IPS driver.

KO-KO., POOH-BAH., and PITTI-SING. An IPS driver!

CEO. Yes; would it be troubling you too much if I asked you to produce him? He goes by the name of----

KATISHA. Nanki-Poo.

CEO. Nanki-Poo.

KO-KO. It's quite easy. That is, it's rather difficult. In point of fact, he's gone overseas!

CEO. Gone overseas! Where?

KO-KO. Shangri-La!

KATISHA. (*who is reading certificate of death*). Oh No!

CEO. What's the matter?

KATISHA. Look--his name--Nanki-Poo--terminated this morning. Oh, where shall I find him? Where will I find another?

[*Ko-Ko, Pooh-Bah, and Pitti-Sing fall on their knees.*]

CEO. (*looking at paper*). Dear, dear, dear! This is very tiresome. (*To Ko-Ko.*) My poor fellow, in your anxiety to carry out my wishes you have fired the *heir to the Chairman of the Board*!

KO-KO. I beg to offer an unqualified apology.

POOH-BAH. Ah…me too!

PITTI-SING. We really hadn't no idea--

CEO. Of course not. How could you? Come, come, my good fellow, don't worry yourself--it was no fault of yours. If a man with a guaranteed seat on the Board of Directors chooses to disguise himself as an IPS driver, he has to take the consequences. It really distresses me to see you take on so. I have no doubt he thoroughly deserved all he got. (*They rise.*)

KO-KO. We are infinitely obliged, Sir----

PITTI-SING. Much obliged, Sir.

POOH-BAH. Very much obliged, Sir.

CEO. Obliged? not a bit. Don't mention it. How could you tell?

POOH-BAH. No, of course we couldn't tell who the man really was.

PITTI-SING. It wasn't written on his forehead, you know. Ha! ha! ha!

KO-KO. Ha! ha! ha!

CEO. Ha! ha! ha! (*To Katisha.*) I forget the disciplinary policy for firing the boss' son.

KO-KO., POOH-BAH, and PITTI-SING. Disciplinary policy! (*They drop down on their knees again.*)

CEO. Yes. Something lingering, with lots of aggravation and frustration in it, I imagine. Something like that. I think it has to do with keeping Windows7.0® up and running, but I'm not sure. I know it's something humorous, but lingering, with either correcting AP Tests or interning at Dunkin Donuts, but don't worry. I'm not a bit angry.

KO-KO. (*in abject terror*). If you will accept our assurance, we had no idea----

CEO. Of course----

PITTI-SING. I knew nothing about it.

POOH-BAH. I wasn't there.

CEO. That's the pathetic part of it. Unfortunately, the fool of a policy says "firing the boss's son." There's not a word about a mistake-- KO-KO., PITTI-SING., and POOH-BAH. No!

CEO. Or not knowing----

KO-KO. No!

CEO. Or having no notion----

PITTI-SING. No!

CEO. Or not being there----

POOH-BAH. No!

CEO. There should be, of course---

KO-KO., PITTI-SING., and POOH-BAH. YES!

CEO. But there isn't.

KO-KO., PITTI-SING., and POOH-BAH. OH!

CEO. That's the sloppy way these policies are always drawn up. But, cheer up, it'll be all right. I'll have it altered next year. Now, let's see about your disciplinary procedure—will after lunch suit you? Can you wait till then?

KO-KO., PITTI-SING., and POOH-BAH. Oh, yes--*we can wait* till then!

CEO. Then we'll make it after lunch.

POOH-BAH. I don't want any lunch.

CEO. I'm really very sorry for you all, but it's an unfair world, and virtue is triumphant only in the theatre.

GLEE.--PITTI-SING, KATISHA, KO-KO, POOH-BAH and CEO,

CEO. SEE HOW THE FATES THEIR GIFTS ALLOT,
FOR A IS HAPPY--B IS NOT.
YET B IS WORTHY, I DARE SAY,
OF MORE PROSPERITY THAN A!

KO-KO., POOH-BAH., AND PITTI-SING.
IS B MORE WORTHY?

KATISHA. I SHOULD SAY HE'S WORTH A GREAT DEAL MORE THAN A.

ENSEMBLE: YET A IS HAPPY!

OH, SO HAPPY!
LAUGHING, HA! HA!
CHAFFING, HA! HA!
NECTAR QUAFFING, HA! HA! HA!
EVER JOYOUS, I SHOULD SAY,
HAPPY, UNDESERVING A!

KO-KO., POOH-BAH., AND PITTI-SING.

IF I WERE FORTUNE--WHICH I'M NOT--
B SHOULD ENJOY A'S HAPPY LOT,
AND A SHOULD DIE IN MISERY--
THAT IS, ASSUMING I AM B.

CEO. AND KATISHA. BUT SHOULD A PERISH?

KO-KO., POOH-BAH., AND PITTI-SING.

THAT SHOULD BE
(OF COURSE, ASSUMING I AM B).
B SHOULD BE HAPPY!
OH, SO HAPPY!
LAUGHING, HA! HA!
CHAFFING, HA! HA!
NECTAR QUAFFING, HA! HA! HA!
BUT CONDEMNED TO GO IS HE,
WRETCHED MERITORIOUS B!

[*Exit CEO and Katisha.*]

KO-KO. Well, a nice mess you've got us into, with your nodding head and the deference due to a man of high status!

POOH-BAH. Merely adding detail to lend an air of realism to a pathetic lie you were making up.

PITTI-SING. Details! Detail bologna!

KO-KO. And you're just as bad as *he* is with your stupid story about catching his eye and his whistling a song. But that's so like you! You have to put your nose into everything!

POOH-BAH. But how about you - baring your teeth?

PITTI-SING. Yes, and your Waterman® pen!

KO-KO. Well, well, never mind that now. There's only one thing to be done. Nanki-Poo hasn't left yet--he must come back at once. (*Enter Nanki-Poo and Yum-Yum prepared for journey.*) Here he comes. Here, Nanki-Poo, I've good news for you--you're rehired.

NANKI-POO. Oh, but it's too late. I'm a happily unemployed man, and I'm off for my honeymoon.

KO-KO. Nonsense! A terrible thing has just happened. Come to find out, you're the son of the CEO!

NANKI-POO. Yes, but that happened some time ago.

KO-KO. Is this a time for clever, tongue in cheek humor that mostly goes over the audiences head?? I think not! Your father is here, and with Katisha!

NANKI-POO. My father! And with Katisha!

KO-KO. Yes, he wants you particularly.

POOH-BAH. So does *she*.

YUM-YUM. Oh, but he's *married* now.

KO-KO. But, bless my heart! What does that have to do with anything?

NANKI-POO. Katisha claims betrothal with me – you know – betrothal – it's an ancient pre-marital status that implies a bond without there actually being a marriage covenant . . . I see you scratch your heads. Never mind. The bad news is, I can't marry her because I'm married already—consequently, according to the Mikado Enterprises, LLC Discipline Policy Manual, Chapter 13, Section 4, Paragraph 10, she's entitled to insist on my shredding, my wife will have to be drowned in White-Out®. . .

YUM-YUM. . . . according to the Mikado Enterprises, LLC Discipline Policy Manual, Chapter 13, Section 4, Paragraph 12.5, (when an employee is shredded, his wife, if also employed, is to be drowned in a vat of White-Out®). . .You see our difficulty.

KO-KO. Yes. I don't know what's to be done.

NANKI-POO. There's one chance for you. If you can persuade Katisha to marry *you*, she would have no further claim on me, and in that case I could come back to work at Mikado Enterprises, L.L.C. without any fear of the shredder.

YUM-YUM. Or the White-Out®.

KO-KO. If *I* marry *Katisha*!!

YUM-YUM. I really think it's the only way to go.

KO-KO. But, my goodness, haven't you seen her? She's disgusting!

PITTI-SING. Oh! that's only her *face*. She features her left elbow on her own teice weekly webcam show!

POOH-BAH. On the internet! [*They giggle.*]

KO-KO. Sir, I refuse to marry anyone with a webcam show!

NANKI-POO. It comes to this: While Katisha is single, I prefer to be unemployed. When Katisha is married, re-employment will be as welcome as the flowers in spring!

DUET--NANKI-POO and KO-KO. (*With YUM-YUM, PITTI-SING, and POOH-BAH.*)

NANKI-POO.

THE FLOWERS THAT BLOOM IN THE SPRING, TRA LA,
BREATHE PROMISE OF MERRY SUNSHINE--
AS WE MERRILY DANCE AND WE SING, TRA LA,
WE WELCOME THE HOPE THAT THEY BRING, TRA LA,
OF A SUMMER OF ROSES AND WINE.
AND THAT'S WHAT WE MEAN WHEN WE SAY
THAT A THING
IS WELCOME AS FLOWERS THAT BLOOM IN THE SPRING.
TRA LA LA LA LA LA, ETC.

ALL. TRA LA LA LA, ETC.

KO-KO. THE FLOWERS THAT BLOOM IN THE SPRING, TRA LA,
HAVE NOTHING TO DO WITH THE CASE.
I'VE GOT TO TAKE UNDER MY WING, TRA LA,
A MOST UNATTRACTIVE OLD THING, TRA LA,
WITH A CARICATURE OF A FACE
AND THAT'S WHAT I MEAN WHEN I SAY, OR I SING,
"OH, BOTHER THE FLOWERS THAT BLOOM IN THE
SPRING."
TRA LA LA LA LA LA, ETC.

ALL. TRA LA LA LA, TRA LA LA LA, ETC.

[*Dance and exeunt Nanki-Poo, Yum-Yum, Pooh-Bah, Pitti-Sing, and Ko-Ko. Enter Katisha.*]

RECITATIVE and SONG.--KATISHA.

ALONE, AND YET ALIVE! OH, SEPULCHRE!
MY SOUL IS STILL MY BODY'S PRISONER!
REMOTE THE PEACE THAT DEATH ALONE CAN GIVE--
MY DOOM, TO WAIT! MY PUNISHMENT, TO LIVE!

SONG.

HEARTS DO NOT BREAK! THEY STING AND ACHE
FOR OLD LOVE'S SAKE, BUT DO NOT DIE,
THOUGH WITH EACH BREATH THEY LONG FOR DEATH
AS WITNESSETH THE LIVING I!
OH, LIVING I! COME, TELL ME WHY,
WHEN HOPE IS GONE, DO YOU STAY ON?
WHY LINGER HERE, WHERE ALL IS DREAR?
OH, LIVING I! COME, TELL ME WHY,
WHEN HOPE IS GONE, DO YOU STAY ON?
MAY NOT A CHEATED MAIDEN DIE?

KO-KO. (*entering and approaching her timidly*). Katisha!

KATISHA. The criminal who robbed me of my love! But vengeance will be mine after lunch!

KO-KO. Katisha—behold, I worship at your feet! Katisha—have mercy!

KATISHA. Mercy? Did you mercy on him? See here, you! You have terminated my love. He did not love me yet, but he would have loved me eventually. Katisha is an acquired taste--only the educated palate can appreciate me. I was educating *his* palate when he ran away from me. Well, he's been fired, and where will I find another? It takes years to train a co-worker to love me. Am I to go through all that effort again, and, at the same time, find mercy in my heart for you, the clueless functionary who robbed me of my prey--I mean my pupil--just as his education was on the point of completion? Oh, where will I find another?

KO-KO. (*suddenly, and with great vehemence, indicating himself*). Here!--Here!

KATISHA. What!!!

KO-KO. (*with intense passion*). Katisha, for years I have loved you with a white-hot passion that is slowly but surely eating me from the inside out! Don't shrink from me! If you have any cleaning woman's mercy in your heart, don't spurn these advances of a love-sick worshipper. Oh how I thrill when you whip out your feather duster! Oh how the way you thrust your plunger excites! Oh how you have mopped up my hidden devotion and wrung it in your love bucket all these years!! (*lower*) My push broom thrills at your tiniest touch! I see you bristle at my advances… it's true that for years I have tried, weakly, to conceal my fiery passion which really fries my aspirations for you - but the fire will not be smothered!—it defies all attempts to put out – put it out. Katisha, I dare not hope for your love--but I will not live without it! Darling!

KATISHA. You, whose hands signed the termination papers of my betrothed, dare to address words of passion to the woman you have so foully wronged!

KO-KO. I do--accept my love, or I perish on the spot!

KATISHA. Perish, then. Who knows better than I that a broken heart won't kill you?!

KO-KO. You don't know what you are saying. Listen!

SONG--KO-KO-KO-KO.

ON A TREE BY A RIVER A LITTLE TOM-TIT
SANG "WILLOW, TITWILLOW, TITWILLOW!"
AND I SAID TO HIM, "DICKY-BIRD, WHY DO YOU SIT
SINGING WILLOW, TITWILLOW, TITWILLOW'?"
"IS IT WEAKNESS OF INTELLECT, BIRDIE?" I CRIED,
"OR A RATHER TOUGH WORM IN YOUR LITTLE INSIDE?"
WITH A SHAKE OF HIS POOR LITTLE HEAD, HE REPLIED,
"OH, WILLOW, TITWILLOW, TITWILLOW!"

HE SLAPPED AT HIS CHEST, AS HE SAT ON THAT BOUGH,
SINGING "WILLOW, TITWILLOW, TITWILLOW!"
AND A COLD PERSPIRATION BESPANGLED HIS BROW,
OH, WILLOW, TITWILLOW, TITWILLOW!
HE SOBBED AND HE SIGHED, AND A GURGLE HE GAVE,
THEN HE PLUNGED HIMSELF INTO THE BILLOWY WAVE,
AND AN ECHO AROSE FROM THE SUICIDE'S GRAVE--
"OH, WILLOW, TITWILLOW, TITWILLOW!"

NOW I FEEL JUST AS SURE AS I'M SURE THAT MY NAME
ISN'T WILLOW, TITWILLOW, TITWILLOW,
THAT 'TWAS BLIGHTED AFFECTION
THAT MADE HIM EXCLAIM
"OH, WILLOW, TITWILLOW, TITWILLOW!"
AND IF YOU REMAIN CALLOUS AND OBDURATE, I
SHALL PERISH AS HE DID, AND YOU WILL KNOW WHY,
THOUGH I PROBABLY SHALL NOT EXCLAIM AS I DIE,
"OH, WILLOW, TITWILLOW, TITWILLOW!"

(*During this song Katisha has been greatly saddened, and at the end is almost in tears.*)

KATISHA. (*whimpering*). Did he really die of love?

KO-KO. He really did.

KATISHA. All on account of a cruel little hen?

KO-KO. Yes.

KATISHA. Poor little thing!

KO-KO. It's a sad story - and quite true. I knew the bird intimately.

KATISHA. Did you? He must have been very fond of her.

KO-KO. His devotion was unbelievable.

KATISHA. (*still whimpering*). Poor little thing! And--and if I refuse you, will you go and do the same?

KO-KO. Without hesitation.

KATISHA. No, no--you mustn't! Anything but that! (*Falls on his chest.*) Oh, I'm a silly little goose!

KO-KO. (*making a wry face*). Or something!

KATISHA. And you won't hate me because I'm just a little teeny weeny wee bit bloodthirsty, will you?

KO-KO. Hate you? Oh, Katisha! is there not beauty even in bloodthirstiness?

KATISHA. My idea exactly.

DUET--KATISHA AND KO-KO.

KATISHA. THERE IS BEAUTY IN THE BELLOW OF THE BLAST,
THERE IS GRANDEUR IN THE GROWLING OF THE GALE,
THERE IS ELOQUENT OUTPOURING
WHEN THE LION IS A-ROARING,
AND THE TIGER IS A-LASHING OF HIS TAIL!

KO-KO. YES, I LIKE TO SEE A TIGER
FROM THE CONGO OR THE NIGER,
AND ESPECIALLY WHEN LASHING OF HIS TAIL!

KATISHA. VOLCANOES HAVE A SPLENDOR THAT IS GRIM,
AND EARTHQUAKES ONLY TERRIFY THE DOLTS,
BUT TO HIM WHO'S SCIENTIFIC
THERE'S NOTHING THAT'S TERRIFIC
IN THE FALLING OF A FLIGHT OF THUNDERBOLTS!

KO-KO. YES, IN SPITE OF ALL MY MEEKNESS,
IF I HAVE A LITTLE WEAKNESS,
IT'S A PASSION FOR A FLIGHT OF THUNDERBOLTS!

BOTH. IF THAT IS SO, SING DERRY DOWN DERRY!
IT'S EVIDENT, VERY, OUR TASTES ARE ONE.
AWAY WE'LL GO, AND MERRILY MARRY,
NOR TARDILY TARRY 'TILL DAY IS DONE!

KO-KO. THERE IS BEAUTY IN EXTREME OLD AGE--
DO YOU FANCY YOU ARE ELDERLY ENOUGH?
INFORMATION I'M REQUESTING
ON A SUBJECT INTERESTING:
IS A MAIDEN ALL THE BETTER WHEN SHE'S TOUGH?

KATISHA. THROUGHOUT THIS WIDE DOMINION
IT'S THE GENERAL OPINION
THAT SHE'LL LAST A GOOD DEAL LONGER WHEN SHE'S TOUGH.

KO-KO. ARE YOU OLD ENOUGH TO MARRY, DO YOU THINK?
WON'T YOU WAIT TILL YOU ARE EIGHTY IN THE SHADE?
THERE'S A FASCINATION FRANTIC
IN A RUIN THAT'S ROMANTIC;
DO YOU THINK YOU ARE SUFFICIENTLY DECAYED?

KATISHA. TO THE MATTER THAT YOU MENTION
I HAVE GIVEN SOME ATTENTION,
AND I THINK I AM SUFFICIENTLY DECAYED.

BOTH. IF THAT IS SO, SING DERRY DOWN DERRY!
IT'S EVIDENT, VERY, OUR TASTES ARE ONE!
AWAY WE'LL GO, AND MERRILY MARRY,
NOR TARDILY TARRY 'TILL DAY IS DONE!

[*Exit together. Flourish. Enter the CEO, attended by Pish-Tush and others.*]

CEO. Now then, we've had a capital lunch, and we're quite ready. Have all the painful preparations been made?

PISH-TUSH. All is prepared, Boss.

CEO. Then produce the unfortunate gentleman and his two well-meaning but misguided accomplices.

[*Enter Ko-Ko, Katisha, Pooh-Bah, and Pitti-Sing. They throw themselves at the CEO's feet*]

KATISHA. Mercy! Mercy for Ko-Ko! Mercy for Pitti-Sing! Mercy even for Pooh-Bah!

CEO. I beg your pardon, I don't think I quite caught that remark.

POOH-BAH. Mercy even for Pooh-Bah!!!

KATISHA. Mercy! My husband that was to have been is gone, and I have just married this miserable object.

CEO. Oh! That didn't take you very long!

KO-KO. We caught the Justice of the Peace having a liquid lunch at the Elks.

POOH-BAH. I'm the Justice of the Peace.

CEO. I see. But the trouble is, you have fired the heir to the Chairman of the Board----

[*Enter Nanki-Poo and Yum-Yum.*]

NANKI-POO. The heir to the Chairman of the Board is not fired.

CEO. Bless my heart, my son!

NANKI-POO. Yes, hellooo, Mother…

YUM-YUM. And your daughter-in-law!

KATISHA. (*seizing Ko-Ko*). Traitor, you lied to me! [*wallops him*]

CEO. Yes, you are entitled to an explanation, but I think he will give it better whole than shredded.

KO-KO. It's like this: It is true that I stated that I had terminated Nanki-Poo----

CEO. Yes, with most convincing details.

POOH-BAH. Merely adding detail to lend an air of realism to a pathetic lie they were making up.-

KO-KO. Will you shut up for once? (*To CEO.*) It's like this: When the CEO says, "Do this or that," this or that is as good as done--practically, it is done—because your wish is our command. The CEO says, "Fire a gentleman," and a gentleman is told – "bring your keys to the Vice President of Human Resources". Consequently, that gentleman is as good as fired--practically, he is fired--and if he is practically fired, why not say so?

CEO. I see… [*thinks as everyone watches breathlessly*] … Sounds plausible…

FINALE.

PITTI-SING. For he's gone and married Yum-Yum--
ALL. Yum-Yum!
PITTI-SING. Your anger pray bury,
For all will be merry,
I think you had better succumb--
ALL. Come--come.
PITTI-SING. And join our expressions of glee!
KO-KO. On this subject I pray you be dumb--
ALL Dumb--dumb!
KO-KO. Your notions, though many,
Are not worth a penny,
The word for your guidance is "Mum"--
ALL. Mum--Mum!
KO-KO. You've a very good bargain in me.
ALL. On this subject we pray you be dumb--
Dumb--dumb!
We think you had better succumb--
Come--come!
You'll find there are many
Who'll wed for a penny,
There are lots of good fish in the sea.

YUM-YUM. and NANKI-POO.
The threatened cloud has passed away,
And brightly shines the dawning day;
What though the night may come too
soon, We've years and years of afternoon!
ALL. Then let the throng
Our joy advance,
With laughing song
And merry dance,
With joyous shout and ringing cheer,
Inaugurate our new career!
Then let the throng, etc.

CURTAIN.

Scenery & Costumes:

The board room of Mikado Enterprises, LLC is dominated by a large floor to ceiling window on the 32nd floor of the Mikado Building in the Nihonbashi district of Tokyo. Upstage center is a large conference table surrounded by chairs. The walls feature sales charts (on the decline) and office romance charts (sharply on the increase.)

The ladies' bathroom is the outer room with a powder table and several chairs or benches. It is well appointed and had pink cinderblock walls featuring the international symbol for "Women's Room"

The clothing worn by the actors is all in keeping with contemporary business fashion. The secretaries would wear sneakers, as they are initially leaving work in Scene 6. The "Businessmen of Japan" all have Blackberrys and briefcases.

www.ingramcontent.com/pod-product-compliance
Ingram Content Group UK Ltd.
Pitfield, Milton Keynes, MK11 3LW, UK
UKHW020234250726
13967UKWH00001B/370

9 780557 232543